Clouds

Clouds

By Lucy Haché

Illustrations by Michael Joyal

Winnipeg

Clouds

Book design and layout by Matt Joudrey.

At Bay Press logo copyright © 2015 At Bay Press.

Published by At Bay Press October 2015.

ISBN 978-0-9917610-7-4

Library and Archives Canada cataloguing in publication is available upon request.

Visit At Bay Press online:
atbaypress.com

First Edition

Printed and bound in Canada.

10 9 8 7 6 5 4 3 2 1

To Ryan,
for sharing my world,
storm clouds and all.

I'm surrounded by life.

Above me is the sky in all its shades of blue, grey and white.

There dwell the gulls, ever-moving
yet seemingly suspended in time.

Beneath my back are rocks made smooth
by the pounding of waves.

Then there is the sand: rocks crushed by the ocean's pulse over many days, months or years – who knows what time means to the sea?

Under the sand dwell many creatures such as cockles, butter-clams and horse-clams.

To the North and South the beach stretches
until the forest reaches out to caress it.

To the East is the deep green forest with its ancient cedars, wise spruce and sleepy fir.

The forest is my refuge with all its medicine,
its inhabitants and its vibrancy.

At my feet and to the West is the ever-changing sea.

She's tranquil today and though I'm a lover of storms, I consider her gentleness a gift.

I've come to the edge, where forest meets sea,
to search for answers in the clouds.

As a child I delighted in clouds, seeing in them what I chose: a bear, a whale, a frog. In them I saw kingdoms, worlds to be explored.

My father was a fisherman. To him clouds were messengers –
old-friends who warned him when to take shelter.

As time went on my perception of clouds changed,
much like clouds themselves change.

As a young adult I grew to despise clouds. They were bringers of rain, of sadness, of depression.

I was their captive and felt suffocated
by their oppressive weight.

I spent years bent with the weight of the clouds.

Eventually I realized that I was being oppressed
by my own view of the world.

Like anything, the clouds will reflect
what it is we see in them.

Now they are like friends and I'm thankful
for the many gifts they've given.

After all, my beloved rainforest would not
exist without the generous rain clouds.

Clouds are a mystery and I am studying them.

Perhaps to understand them is to understand myself.

They are intriguing because they are of this world and yet are not. I'm familiar with being of different worlds; my 'Nakwaxda'xw and Scottish-Irish blood waged a war inside me for years, the victor to become my identity.

In the end, I found my identity not in my blood but in the sky, the sea and the forest.

In clouds many see purity, goodness.

Yet there is a clear distinction made between types of clouds: a white fluffy cloud is *good*, a dark purple storm cloud is *bad*.

We have the need to label everything *pretty* or *ugly; right* or *wrong.* As a young woman, I suffered under the weight of these labels, be it *too fat, too tall, too dark, too light* or too anything.

Sometimes I still do.

Maybe I started loving myself when I learned to love storm clouds.

All these thoughts distract me.

I haven't realized the wind has changed.

Storm clouds are gathering above.

A single raindrop falls on my lip, causing a smile to chase contemplation from my face and mind.

As the downpour embraces me,

I am content to just exist.

Glossary of Illustrations: Meteorological Descriptions

Page 1   –   Altostratus
Page 4   –   Cumulonimbus with Lightning
Page 6   –   Mammatus
Page 9   –   Cumulonimbus with Pileus Formation
Page 11 –   Cumulus
Page 14 –   Cirrus
Page 16 –   Cumulonimbus
Page 19 –   Cumulus with display of Crepuscular Rays
Page 20 –   Cumulonimbus
Page 24 –   Cumulonimbus Calvus
Page 27 –   Mammatus
Page 29 –   Cumulus
Page 30 –   Nimbostratus with Pileus Formation
Page 34 –   Cirrocumulus
Page 37 –   Altocumulus
Page 39 –   Cumulonimbus
Page 42 –   Cumulus
Page 45 –   Cumulonimbus
Page 48 –   Cumulus
Page 52 –   Cumulus

About the Author

Lucy Haché, British Columbia based writer and adventurer of First Nations/Métis and Scottish/Irish descent. She grew up in Tsulquate, a small First Nations Community on the Northern tip of Vancouver Island. Much of her childhood was spent in the forest or on the sea. When she's not surrounded by nature she writes about it. She also writes about contemporary and historical First Nations issues.

About the Artist

Michael Joyal, Winnipeg based artist. He recently spent each day of one year drawing a single piece of art, culminating in the show '365 Days Before I Sleep' at Cre8ery Gallery. He has also produced the comic zines 'CrUDE' and 'Disturb'. Mr. Joyal received his BFA from the Nova Scotia College of Art & Design. His work can been seen at leadvitamins.blogspot.com

Other Titles from At Bay Press

Available now:

The Edge 125 Pacific Avenue
Various contributors
Non-Fiction
Paperback
ISBN: 9780987966551
$15.99

At Bay Press Fiction Annual: Jilted Love
Fiction Anthology
Paperback
ISBN: 9780991761005
$9.99

Woman An Anthology
Fiction Anthology
Hardcover
ISBN: 9780991761036
$29.99

Charleswood Road Stories
M C Joudrey
Fiction Stories
Hardcover
ISBN: 9780991761043
$22.99

Forthcoming:

At Bay Press Fiction Annual: Dreams and Nightmares
Fiction Anthology
Paperback
ISBN: 9780991761050
$14.95
Releases: Fall 2015